Library of Congress Cataloging-in-Publication Data

Gyllenhaal, Rebecca, adapter. | Smith, Kim, 1986- illustrator.

Doctor Who : the runaway Tardis / story by Rebecca Gyllenhaal; based on the series created by Chris Chibnall; illustrated by Kim Smith.

LCSH: Doctor (Fictitious character)—Juvenile fiction. | Time travel—Juvenile fiction. | CYAC: Doctor (Fictitious character)—Fiction.

PZ7.1.G95 Doc 2020

DDC [E]—dc2 2019037592

ISBN: 978-1-68369-184-6

Printed in Singapore

Typeset in Miller and Gill Sans

Story by Rebecca Gyllenhaal

Designed by Elissa Flanigan

Production management by John J. McGurk

Quirk Books

215 Church Street

Philadelphia, PA 19106

quirkbooks.com

10 9 8 7 6 5 4 3 2 1

BBC

DOCTOR WHO

THE RUNAWAY TARDIS

Based on the series by Chris Chibnall

Illustrated by Kim Smith

QUIRK BOOKS
PHILADELPHIA

It was Lizzie's first day at her new school.

She didn't know any of the other kids.

So at lunchtime, she sat at a table by herself.

When Lizzie came home, she made a dozen peanut butter sandwiches and stuffed them into her backpack.

"I hate my new school!" she said to her parents. "I don't have any friends there. I'm running away to be with my old friends."

Lizzie marched into the
woods behind her house.

She wondered how she would find her way back
to her old neighborhood.

Then, she saw something strange in the distance.

It looked like a big blue box.
What could it be?

Lizzie pushed the door open
and peered inside.

The box was bigger on the inside!

In the center of the room was a control panel covered in buttons and levers and dials. Lizzie stood on her tip-toes to look at the controls . . . and dropped her sandwich down a slot!

Suddenly, the door swung open with a crash! Lizzie curled up under the control panel to hide.

Lizzie saw a woman wearing a long coat stride into the room.

She pressed a button, pulled a lever, and spun a dial.
A strange sound filled the air.

Suddenly, the floor shook! Red lights flashed!
An alarm blared! Lizzie rolled out from
underneath the control panel.

The Doctor opened the TARDIS door . . .

. . . and Lizzie saw that they were in outer space!

The TARDIS is malfunctioning!
I meant to go to the Silfrax Galaxy, not the
Brouhaha-Nine-Nine-Five Galaxy!
Is this a spaceship?

Of course not!
It's a time *and* spaceship.
If this is a spaceship, does
that mean you're an alien?

The Doctor pressed a big red button, and when she opened the door again . . .

. . . they were in the middle of a field full of dinosaurs!

"Brilliant!" said the Doctor.

"Get us out of here!" said Lizzie.

POLICE PUBLIC CALL BOX
POLICE PUBLIC CALL BOX

The Doctor pressed the button again. This time when she opened the door, they were in Egypt. Lizzie recognized the pyramids and the Great Sphinx from her history books.

Next, the TARDIS traveled to a coral reef in a tropical sea.
Lizzie counted the fish as they swam past the window.
She had never seen so many different kinds!

Finally, the TARDIS landed on the surface of an alien planet.

"Brilliant!" said the Doctor.
"This is Planet Plorp. The Glorp are fantastic engineers. They'll be able to help us fix the TARDIS."

The Doctor and the Glorp got to work.
The Glorp brought their tools into the TARDIS,
and the air rang with sounds of sawing, hammering,
and drilling. Lizzie and the smallest alien, Blorp,
watched them work.

No, that won't do at all!
This thing just won't come off!
Can you hand me one of those wibbly wobbly bits?

“Something in your bag smells delicious,” said Blorp.

“I packed sandwiches,” said Lizzie. “Want one?”

“This is the best thing I’ve ever tasted!” said Blorp.

Suddenly, everyone stopped working.

Something was wrong.

"We need to reverse the polarity of the time configurator," the Doctor said, "and I can't do that without a neutron flow convertor. We'd have to go halfway across the galaxy to find one of those!"

But Lizzie had an idea.
I know how to fix the TARDIS!

Lizzie held Blorp over the control panel.

Blorp was the only one small enough to squeeze into the slot.

Blorp followed the smell to the sandwich and ate it up in two giant bites.

The Doctor pressed a button, pulled a lever, and spun a dial.

A strange sound filled the air: *VWORP VWORP VWORP*.

No alarms blared. No red lights flashed.

“Brilliant!” said the Doctor. “You fixed the TARDIS!”

It was time for Lizzie to go home. Everyone hugged goodbye.

Goodbye, Blorp.
Goodbye, Lizzie. I wish I could go to Earth with you.
POLICE PUBLIC CALL BOX

Lizzie was sad to be leaving the Doctor and the Glorp behind.

"You know, Lizzie," said the Doctor, "I travel through space and time helping people, so I have to say goodbye to old friends all the time. I know how hard it is to start over."

"Do you ever get lonely?" Lizzie asked.

"Everyone gets lonely sometimes," said the Doctor.
"But I make new friends wherever I go,
and I never forget the old ones."

Goodbye, Doctor.
Goodbye, Lizzie.

When the Doctor opened the TARDIS doors, Lizzie was amazed to find that no time had passed. She ran home as quickly as she could.

“We thought you were running away,” said Lizzie’s mother.

“I did run away!” said Lizzie. “And I made friends with the Doctor and the Glorp from Planet Plorp. I guess making human friends at my new school won’t be so hard after all.”

Lizzie ran up to her bedroom and unzipped her backpack.
Inside was one last peanut butter sandwich . . . and Blorp!
They split the sandwich and had the best sleepover ever.